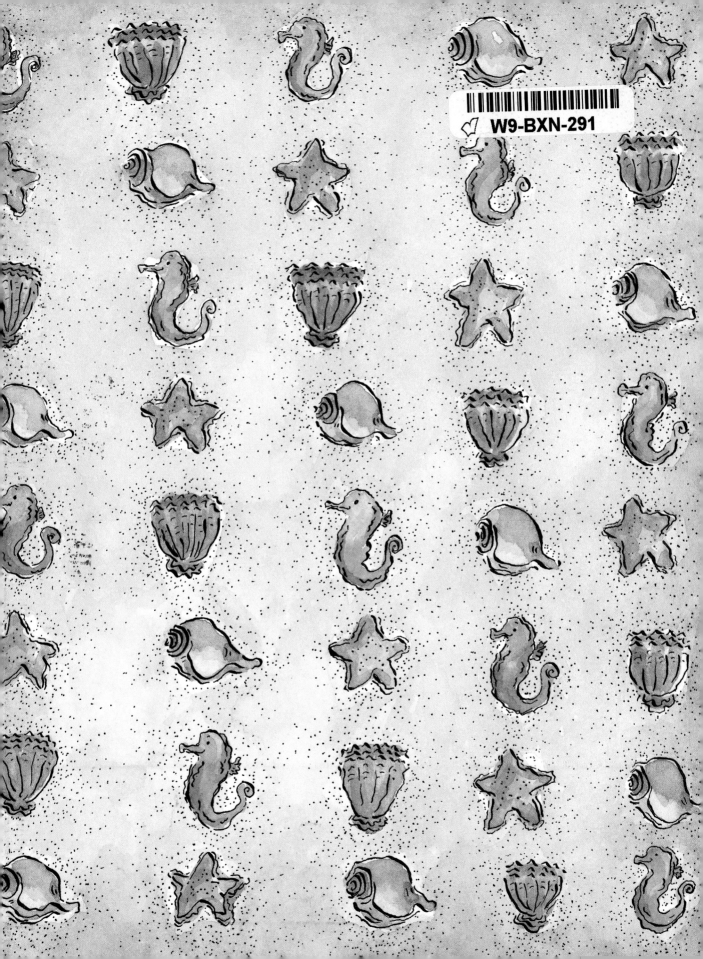

# JOSEPHINA

## THE GREAT COLLECTOR

## DIANA ENGEL

Morrow Junior Books
New York

Inquiries should be addressed to
William Morrow and Company, Inc.,
105 Madison Avenue,
New York, NY 10016.
Printed in Hong Kong.
1  2  3  4  5  6  7  8  9  10
Library of Congress Cataloging in Publication Data
Engel, Diana.
Josephina the great collector.
Summary: Josephina's passion for collecting anything
and everything finally drives her sister out of the room
they both share.
[1. Collectors and collecting—Fiction. 2. Sisters—
Fiction] I. Title.
PZ7.E69874Jo  1988     [E]        87-20358
ISBN 0-688-07542-8
ISBN 0-688-07543-6 (lib. bdg.)

For my father, the greatest collector of all,
and for George, whose distinctive
laughter I hear throughout these pages

Josephina lived in a small house with her large family.

She and her sister, Rose, spent many afternoons together playing,

until . . .

. . . Josephina started to *collect:* anything and everything.
Rose went collecting only once.

After that, Josephina spent more and more time collecting alone.

For her, the world was full of treasures just waiting to be seen and held

and kept.

As Josephina's collection grew bigger and bigger, Rose grew grumpier and grumpier.

But Josephina had never been happier. At night before
bedtime, she looked through her treasures, sometimes
remembering the place where she had found each one.

Rose felt things had gone too far.

"Something has got to be done with all that repulsive junk," she said.

"It's not junk!" Josephina answered loudly.

"Can't you throw *some* of it out?" asked Rose.

"Throw out my very own special, private collection?" Josephina stared at her, wide-eyed.

"Well," suggested Rose, "if you can't throw it out, how about lending it out?"

Josephina thought long and hard.

The next morning, the sisters carried
two boxes of carefully selected items to their
Uncle Mario's house around the corner.

At least I can still see these things when-
ever I want, thought Josephina.

Mario was their favorite uncle and quite a collector himself.

His nieces were greeted with open arms and the smell of fresh-baked biscuits.

"Sure, sure," said Uncle Mario. "I'll keep an eye on these things for you. Put them in a safe place and then come out back for tea."

While her uncle boiled water,
Josephina looked around with
her collector's eye.

I've always wanted one of these,
she thought, and I could really use
one of these . . . "And this," she said
out loud, "this I just love."

Before she knew it, Josephina had
collected a great pile around her.

Uncle Mario noticed how long it took Josephina to join
them.

"If you see anything in the house," he said, "you want it,
you take it. You know me. I always come up with new
stuff."

"How many sugars, Rose?" he asked.

The girls stumbled home under their heavy loads. Rose
was more discouraged than ever.
"I knew it wouldn't be that easy," she muttered to herself.

That night, the sisters got ready for bed. Rose looked
around and sighed.

"I give up!" she said, and she trudged downstairs to sleep
on the living room couch.

Josephina took out a box of her best shells. The room
seemed awfully quiet without Rose.

Amidst the clutter, she lay awake in the dark . . . alone.
Finally, Josephina fell asleep, but she woke early the next
morning with a wonderful idea.

Quietly, in the hush before dawn, Josephina brought up a
box of tools from the cellar.
    She carried her collection downstairs, piece by precious
piece, and grabbed anything else that might be useful.

Then she started to work.

And work . . .

And work . . .

"Breakfast!" her mother called, just as Josephina finished.

"I have a big surprise," Josephina said at the table. "It's in the backyard."

"Oh no!" groaned Rose.

Josephina led the whole family outside
to their old playhouse.
Even Rose was impressed.

"Out of all that junk, you've made a masterpiece,"
she said. "It doesn't even smell too bad!"

"And you know," said Josephina, "it's just big enough for two!"

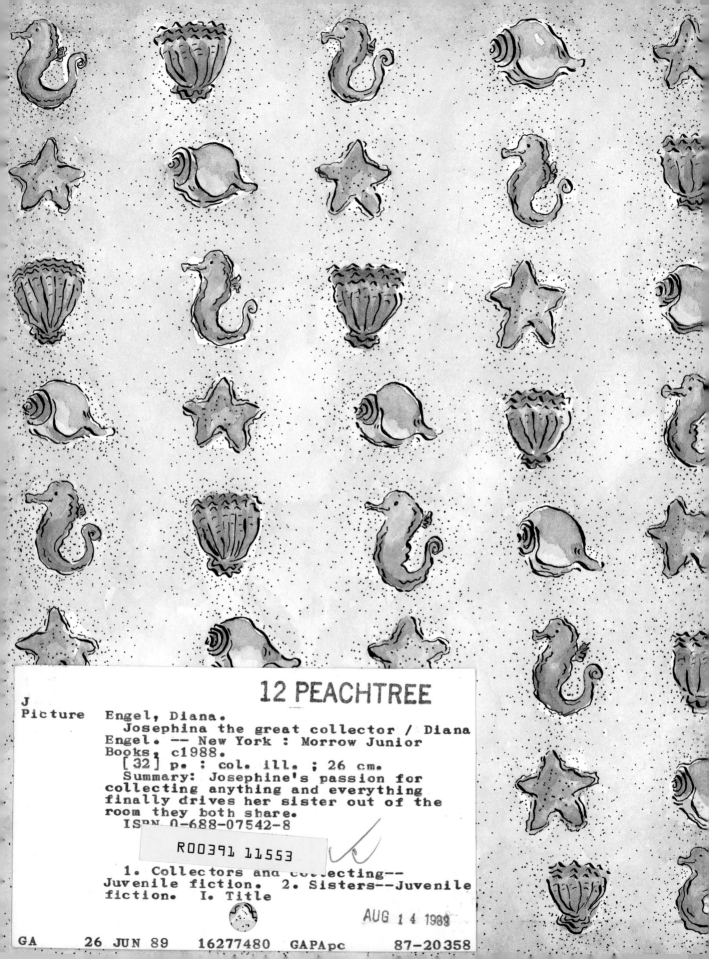